KNIT, KNIT, KNIT, KNIT

Polly Peebles liked to knit.
She liked to knit things
that someone could wear.
Knit, knit, knit, knit.

Every week,
her friend Sara
came to visit.
"What are you knitting now?"
she asked.

"Socks for my brother,"
said Polly Peebles.
"I like to knit things
that someone can wear."
Knit, knit, knit, knit.

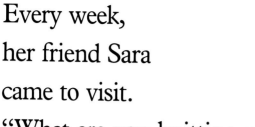

Polly Peebles knitted
so much and so fast
that soon everyone had
all the knitted things they needed.

But Polly Peebles had lots of leftover yarn.

9

Next week,
when Sara came to visit,
Polly Peebles was knitting
something very long.
"Who is that for?" asked Sara.

"I don't know," said Polly Peebles.
"Everyone I know has a scarf.
But what else could I knit
with so many bits
of leftover yarn?"
Knit, knit, knit, knit.

Next week,
when Sara came to visit,
Polly Peebles was knitting
some very long socks.
"Who is going to wear them?"
said Sara.

Polly Peebles smiled.

"George is going to wear them,"
she said.
"I got a new pet to wear my scarf.
Now I'm knitting him some socks.

14

"I like to knit things
that someone can wear."
Knit, knit, knit, knit.

16